MAMA REX AND T

Turn Off the TV

by Rachel Vail

illustrations by Steve Björkman

SCHOLASTIC INC.
New York Toronto London Auckland Sydney
Mexico City New Delhi Hong Kong Buenos Aires

To Jill, my friend through darkness and light.
—RV

To Matthew Gross, with love.
—SB

ISBN 0-439-32176-X

Text copyright © 2002 by Rachel Vail.
Art copyright © 2002 by Steve Björkman.

All rights reserved. Published by Scholastic Inc.
SCHOLASTIC and associated logos are trademarks and/or
registered trademarks of Scholastic Inc.
Lego is a registered trademark of KIRKBI AG.

12 11 10 9 8 7 6 5 4 3 2   2 3 4 5 6 7/0

Book design by Chad W. Beckerman

Printed in the U.S.A.
First Scholastic printing, February 2002

Contents

Chapter 1
TELEVISION

It was a dark and stormy day.

T woke up early and watched the lightning out his window.

He was excited.

It was Saturday and he couldn't play outside.

Mama Rex couldn't bring him on any errands.

T was going to watch TV all day long.

T pulled on his slippers and padded to the living room.

He sat on the couch, picked up the remote, and turned on the TV.

It was the news.

There was a problem with garbage bags someplace.

The bags kept breaking and garbage was falling into people's shoes.

   Mama Rex had been sleeping through the
pounding rain.
   She slept through the lightning and the thunder.
   She woke up from the noise of T's laughter.
   She blinked, saw the storm, and heard
more laughing from the living room.
   Mama Rex yanked on her bathrobe and
went to investigate.

"What are you watching?" asked Mama Rex, rubbing her eyes.

"The news," said T. "It's funny."

"Funny?" said Mama Rex. "I'm going to get some coffee. What a storm, huh?"

T switched channels.

He watched a music video, a little bit of what the weather was in South America, the last minute of a cartoon, and eleven commercials.

Mama Rex brought T two waffles, with syrup.

"What should we do today?" Mama Rex asked T. But T was not hearing her.

He was watching some people sitting on a
couch, sipping coffee from mugs. Their mugs were
not as beautiful as Mama Rex's mug.
  The people were not his mother.
  He had no idea what they were talking about.
  It sounded like blah, blah, blah.
  But T watched and watched.

Mama Rex sat next to T and watched, also.
T sank into the couch, deeper and deeper.
His mouth was hanging open.
His waffles were getting cold.
Mama Rex's coffee was getting cold, too.

A commercial came on.

"Mama Rex!" yelled T. He pointed at the TV.

"Can we get some of that?"

"Car oil?" asked Mama Rex.

"Listen," said T. "It's the best for your car."

"T," said Mama Rex. "We don't even have a car."

"Oh, yeah," said T.

The commercial ended.
Mama Rex and T stared straight ahead,
watching.
Mama Rex pointed at the next commercial.
"Maybe we should buy that," said Mama Rex.
"We want the best for our cat."
"Uh, Mama Rex?" asked T. "What cat?"
"Oh, yeah," said Mama Rex. "No cat."

A commercial began for baby diapers.
Mama Rex and T both opened their mouths.
They both pointed at the television.
They turned to each other and both said,
"Hey!"
Then they both smiled and said, "Oh, yeah.
No baby."

After a while, Mama Rex and T looked like part of the couch. T's body was slumped in the corner like an old pillow.

The remote had slipped from his hand and fallen on the floor.

Their eyes were huge and glassy, like little televisions.

Mama Rex and T were becoming furniture.

T switched channels. A show came on.
There were people and animals running around.
    Mama Rex and T didn't really know what was happening.
    But outside it was dark and stormy, so they just sat and watched.

Suddenly the TV turned off.

The lights went out.

The only noise was rain, tapping against the windows.

T sat up. "What happened?"

Mama Rex and T looked around.

"It's a blackout," said Mama Rex. "Lightning knocked out the power."

"No TV?" asked T. "What are we supposed to do?"

Chapter 2
IN THE DARK

A bolt of lightning lit up the room. Afterwards it was dark again.

Mama Rex counted, "One, two, three, four, five . . ." *KA-BOOM!* went the thunder.

"What were you counting?" asked T.

"You count from lightning to thunder to see how far away the storm is," explained Mama Rex.

"And how far is it?" asked T.

"Um," said Mama Rex. "Five! Should we look for a flashlight?"

"Yeah!" yelled T.

Mama Rex and T went to the hall closet.
They found a bicycle pump, T's scooter, four helmets, six phone books, and seven umbrellas.
No flashlight.

"Maybe in my toy box," suggested T.

"Great idea," said Mama Rex, following him.

T opened his toy box and dug in. He found four markers, three marker caps, lots of blocks, another helmet, eight toy cars, and fifteen plastic little friends.

But no flashlight.

"Boy, we haven't built anything together in a long time," said Mama Rex, stacking one block on top of another.

"That looks good," said T. He added rectangular blocks on the sides. "We could put the little friends on it. It could be their something. Town or castle or garbage dump."

Mama Rex was splayed on the floor, sticking her tongue out in concentration. She liked the fancy blocks best.

T liked the rectangles.

A flash of lightning lit up their block structure. It looked really dramatic.

T counted with Mama Rex this time: "One, two, three, four, five . . ."

KA-BOOM!

"Still five away," said T. "And we haven't found a flashlight!"

Mama Rex grunted, pushing herself up. "Maybe in the kitchen," she said.

Following her down the hall, T said, "Walter's mother keeps the flashlight in the flashlight drawer."

"Does she?" asked Mama Rex. "How nice."

Mama Rex opened the junk drawer.

T rummaged through. He found baggie ties, birthday candles, three googly eyes, a "W" magnet, and a Lego guy's head.

No flashlight.

He sat down on the floor. "There's nothing to do," moaned T. "I'm bored."

T lay down on the kitchen floor.
Under the cabinet was a dark lump. T grabbed it.
It was — a flashlight!
"Hooray!" yelled T.
He pushed the switch to shine it at Mama Rex.
Nothing.
"Hey," said T.
"Bummer," said Mama Rex. "Dead batteries.
But I think we have more."
"Hoo . . ." started T, but stopped himself before
". . . ray."
"Where?" he asked. "What if we can't ever
find them?"

Mama Rex smiled. "Walter's mother may have a flashlight drawer," she said. "But I have a battery bin."

Mama Rex opened the refrigerator.

She lifted the door marked "Cheese." Three packages of batteries tumbled out onto the floor.

"Hooray!" yelled T.

Mama Rex and T loaded fresh batteries into the flashlight.

The flashlight shined bright and strong.

T pointed it into the refrigerator. "Hey," he said. "It's dark in there."

Mama Rex slapped herself on the forehead.
"The electricity is off, so the refrigerator
is off."
"All the food will spoil!" yelled T.
"Unless we eat it first," said Mama Rex.

Mama Rex and T had a feast on the kitchen floor. They spread a tablecloth over the tiles, and stood the flashlight on its bottom.

They ate chicken and ice cream and ice pops and leftover pizza and butter, until they were stuffed.

Lightning lit the remains of their feast.
"One, two, three, four, five, six . . ."
KA-BOOM!
"Getting farther," said T, looking out the window
at the rain. "Going away."
Mama Rex stood beside him. "I'm sure glad
we're not in a tent somewhere," she said.

"A tent!" yelled T. "Let's make a tent in the living room!"

"OK," said Mama Rex.

T dragged the tablecloth behind him, and stretched it from the couch to the coffee table.

Mama Rex and T crawled under.

They sat in their tent whispering stories to each other by flashlight.

Until they heard very loud noises.

Chapter 3
BRIGHT AND NOISY

"What was that?" T whispered, holding onto Mama Rex.

Mama Rex poked her head out of their tent. She started to laugh.

T opened his eyes. He poked his head out, too.

Out in the living room, it was bright and noisy. The lights were on and the TV was blaring.

T jumped up and toppled the tent. "Hooray!" he yelled. "The blackout is over! We can have fun again!"

Mama Rex smiled. She pushed herself up off the floor and onto the couch.

T turned off his flashlight and plopped down beside her.

They watched a commercial for hamburgers.

"Ugh," said T. "That looks disgusting." He leaned back against the couch.

They watched a commercial for stuff to make rugs smell better.

Mama Rex looked at T.

T looked at Mama Rex.

T picked up the remote control and pressed the power button. The TV flashed off.

T smiled and started counting. "One, two, three, four, five, six, seven . . ." *Ka-boom!*

"Very far away," said Mama Rex, spreading the tablecloth from the couch to the table.

"Good," said T. He clicked his flashlight on and together they crawled back inside the tent.